ELD
Pw

This book was published by Stewed Rhubarb Press
in November 2018, with the ISBN number
978-1-910416-10-5.

Editor
Angie Spoto

Internal illustrations
Brian Houston
www.createpod.com

Typesetting, layout and cover
James T. Harding
www.james-t-harding.com

The Positive Stories project was hosted by HIV Scotland and
kindly supported by the Scottish Graduate School of Arts and
Humanities, as well as Gilead Sciences who provided funding
www.hivscotland.com

Workshop leaders
Colin Herd
Angie Spoto
Peter McCune
Katy Hasty

DISCLOSURES

REWRITING THE NARRATIVE ABOUT HIV

EDITED BY ANGIE SPOTO

RJ ARKHIPOV, MARK CARLISE, KEVIN CROWE,
WILL DALGLEISH, STEPHEN DUFFY, J. WILLIAM JAMES,
MATTHEW LYNCH, JAMES MCABRAHAM, NJ MILLAR,
NOBODY, MICHAEL NUGENT, OLIVER, RIO, FRASER SERLE,
NATHAN SPARLING, ANGIE SPOTO AND JAMIE STEWART

www.stewedrhubarb.org

iv

Foreword by Jackie Kay

Stigma prevents early diagnosis. The power that comes from telling a story allows you to take control of your life, to pass on some of what you wished you knew then, that you do know now, to turn something potentially destructive—stigma, secrecy, shame—into something creative and surprising.

The impulse behind telling a story is the impulse to share. You are your own first reader; you first share your own story with your old self, and in so doing you claim something of yourself back. But just as importantly, you share the story with other readers, with kindred spirits, with people who might find echoes in your story; or with people who haven't experienced what you or your characters are experiencing, whose eyes and ears are opened by the very existence of your story. These stories could not be timelier or more important. As a society, we desperately need to change our story on HIV. We need a whole new narrative. Gone are the days in this country when HIV seemed to mean AIDS in disguise; gone are the days when HIV seemed like a death sentence; and gone are the days when you passed on HIV through having sex. We need to change the story.

Yet the old fears and superstitions and neo-biblical warnings have been woven into the fabric of lies about HIV. Bit by bit, the stories here stitch new squares in the tapestry of stories. We should never underestimate the power of stories to heal and to reveal, to shape and to make, to guide and change the tide. And we must never forget what it costs to share a story—the first steps are always brave ones. Many of the writers included in this anthology are new to writing. They have come with their story in their backpack to a workshop and learnt something about the writing process to craft their story or poem and get it out of the backpack and into the world. We should thank all the people that enable this creative and kind process to happen: the midwives of stories, the birthing assistants of poems, the helpers and the shakers. And we should thank all the people in this book bold enough and brave enough to bring these stories and poems out of the HIV closet and into this Scotland, in all their colourful and diverse glory.

I'm proud to be the Makar of a country that knows the importance of stories and poems such as these, that applauds the pioneers and the game changers.

But most of all I'm delighted to have been asked to write a short foreword to this book, because here are emotionally charged, moving, challenging, beautiful, lyrical stories and poems provoked and inspired by the experience of having HIV. NJ Millar's beautifully written 'Jörmungandr' gets the collection off to a very fine start: a story which explores in detail the tumultuous emotions on first finding out about HIV. Life changed forever, she says, with those three little letters. Mark Carlisle's searing and touching poem about feeling untouchable will strike a chord with readers who have felt the same thing, but he also explores in a short poem the positive ways that the HIV catalyst can provide a key for change. Kevin Crowe's utterly absorbing story moves between the late seventies and today beginning with "yet another World AIDS Day service." 'Víreas' by J. William James is an utterly unusual and totally compelling story of a small boy coming of age in a convent island where a beloved nun has contracted AIDS.

Not only is this collection punctuated with useful advice about medication, disclosure and testing, but the poems and stories often contain words of advice within them like Rio's in her 'Message to My Younger Self': "Don't let the bastards grind you down."

The reader has a strong sense in Angie Spoto's poem 'Ashes of a Visible Girl', and in other stories, of the absence and the presence that HIV causes in people's lives. How the absent are still present with us; and how sometimes the present can be absent. These stories chart the coming to terms with the knowledge of HIV, how to deal with it positively and how to reshape the story for future generations. Stigma will often make people hide away. The uplifting thing about these stories and poems is that the poets and short story writers included here are not hiding anymore.

Jackie Kay, Edinburgh 2018

Editor's Note

Less than a year ago, I knew very little about HIV. I was savvy enough to know HIV couldn't be transmitted by kissing or touching, but I didn't know about PrEP—a pill people who are HIV negative can take to prevent them acquiring HIV—or that people living with HIV who are on effective medication and have a reduced level of virus in their bodies cannot pass on HIV to their sexual partners.

It didn't occur to me that anyone could be affected by HIV, regardless of sexuality, gender, race or social class because I was familiar only with the narrative pervasive in our culture today—that HIV affects only gay men or drug users, people who have contracted the virus in some way due to the 'faults' of their lifestyle. And I still believed HIV was a killer, the harbinger of AIDS, symbolised by the image of a looming black tombstone, that classic advert from the 80s.

This is a false narrative. The landscape of HIV today is vastly different than it was thirty years ago. HIV is no longer a death sentence. Many people with HIV live long, healthy lives. They're mothers and fathers, lovers and activists. They're anyone, and each of their stories is unique.

I joined the team at HIV Scotland as their artist in residence with the goal of reshaping the narrative of HIV through storytelling.

HIV Scotland is a leading policy organisation. With the insight and input of people living with and at risk of HIV, it influences public policy, with campaigns bringing PrEP to NHS Scotland and defining a roadmap for challenging HIV stigma. This book is punctuated by information on the key areas of public policy HIV Scotland advocates for. We hope readers of the collection realise how far HIV policy and treatment have advanced—and how much is left yet to be done.

HIV Scotland recognised the power of creative activism on influencing policy—hence the Positive Stories project was born. As part of this, I organised writing workshops for HIV-positive people as well as a mentorship programme that paired people affected by HIV with professional writers. Many people who attended the workshops and participated in the programme were new writers who knew they had a story to tell but weren't quite sure how to tell it. Many of the pieces in this anthology were born from these workshops and one-on-one writing sessions.

The anthology you now hold is the product of a diverse range of voices, all affected in some way by HIV. Their work takes us far beyond the sinister tombstone on a new journey through a myriad of images: moonlight, cigarettes, onion soup, country music, ocean waves, heartbeats, party dresses and net curtains. They tell a new story of HIV. They reshape the narrative. They redefine what it means to have HIV in Scotland today.

Angie Spoto, Edinburgh 2018

Preface from the Chair of HIV Scotland

Thank you for picking up a copy of *Disclosures*.

This book is the culmination of workshops, mentoring and creative writing by the full diversity of people living with and affected by HIV in Scotland. It is a snapshot of a diverse community still experiencing stigma and isolation.

It is worth remembering that some of the stories that were produced during the project haven't made it on to these pages because some people who took part in our project didn't feel confident enough to put their stories to paper. We still experience stigma, discrimination and fear. Our voices, even when they are heard, remain too often feeble, in the background. We have to shout, just to be heard, but even then, it is difficult not to experience stigma. With stigma comes fear of discrimination and retaliation, a reality that, as a woman living with HIV, I know only too well.

I am really grateful to those who shared their stories in this book and I am grateful to anyone who will find the time to read such personal and powerful stories.

This book and the creative-activism contained within it is the beginning of a new movement, not an endpoint. It is the springboard to promoting more stories and proving that everyone living with HIV in Scotland has a voice and a story that will be rightfully heard. Follow our journey as we emerge from the pages of this book to end HIV-related stigma, and together we can finally get to zero new HIV infections and zero HIV-related deaths in Scotland.

Dr Nicoletta Policek, Edinburgh 2018

Contents

Jörmungandr

NJ Millar

+

The silent killer. The new bogeyman. The real-life made-for-TV schlock horror was now everywhere. Writ large.

If you were looking in the right direction. My gaze was averted.

It's funny—I see those three letters in a steely grey colour. Icy. Chilling. Final. Not that surprising I suppose, given the state-sponsored scaremongering. I was ten years old when it aired and was ushered from the room—too young to understand, but old enough to hear the jokes and feel the fear. To sense the othering. And of course, when the pamphlet eventually came through the letterbox it vanished before it hit the mat. We didn't talk about it. Everything swept neatly under the carpet. That was for other people. Dirty people. Not us.

Those three letters stopped my generation in their tracks. Later and away, when I found my tribe, the story grew darker. Still largely ignored, but a legacy nonetheless. Mostly snatched misinformation and rumour. And fear. Fear that if you weren't careful it could be you next. But on we went. Pretending not to notice. Eventually, our folk legend stopped being passed down. Because if we didn't talk about it, it wouldn't exist. And if it didn't exist we were safe. And it seemed practically forgotten. We glossed over the occasional articles about breakthroughs, and we pretended not to notice the faces that disappeared. We turned the other cheek and hoped there wasn't a bloom bruising on it. Our excuse? It was a university town. People came and went. They moved on. That's all it was. Wasn't it? We pretended not to notice those who had lost the wrong kind of weight—those with a haunted look. And we pretended not to notice when they disappeared. It wasn't that we didn't care—but we were glad. Glad it wasn't us. So of course we knew it was still there. Lingering. Knew, knew shame on you. SHAME. ON. YOU. But I had nothing to worry about. Then.

Then...

Because it was then. The line in the sand had been drawn when I wasn't looking. Then and now.

Before.

And.

After.

Three little words.

Three little letters.

Life changed forever.

Then. Now. That's the joke of it all. It is always now. Tomorrow never dies, does it? Ask the Disappeared.

"We're not supposed to say that." That's what he said. The nurse. He said, "We aren't supposed to say that," right after he told me he was sorry. That was the first time I was angry. Not at him, but at that mentality. It felt inhumane, and the anger grew. Fast. Anger at myself. Mostly. Mind racing. The whatabboutery of it all, the instant fear of the unknown, the dread and disgust spinning out of control.

They say it comes in threes. Three is the magic number. Three blind mice. Three wishes. ABC. 123. Three little letters.

Later, before the shutdown. Before the reboot, while wires were still crossed and everything was a jumbled mess, there came grief. Grief so strong and compelling that it could not be contained in any earthly vessel I was familiar with. It churned and rose, grew and overwhelmed. And was unending. A silent scream became a keen. A howl escaped, echoing from somewhere even further than deep within. I didn't think it would ever stop, this noise I didn't know I was even capable of making. And when it was over, I was on the floor, slumped and stunned, crumpled and broken. Is this it now? Tag. You're it.

And of course the crying does stop. Eventually. And life goes on. But it's different now. And it can never go back. Here to stay. And while night does become day and round and round we go, it is in here. Inside. Living. Growing. Spiralling and spreading. Oh God, please get it out of me. Take it away. And I feel sick at the thought all over again.

It's a corner-of-the-eye terror. It's there. You just can't see it. Try as hard as you might, you are never going to catch it. Catch it. It's caught you. Caught in a trap. *I've* caught it. I think about the time before, the then, and I feel like the girl in the horror film you scream at to run. *Run the hell away! It's gonna get you! How can you be this stupid—WHY DIDN'T YOU RUN!* And BAM. Too late. And now it is inside. Round and round it goes. Inside me. A serpent eating its tail. Glowing and growing.

I imagine it glows. This invader. This unwanted guest.

I imagine it's green.

Green for go. Green is the colour of aliens. A sickly unpleasant green. Like that felt-tip pen no one wanted to use. That's you, that is. Damaged goods. Now you've caught it. Tag. You're it. But it must be red. Blood red.

Eight pints. It sounds like a night out. Pumping. Pulsing. Oozing with each beat of your heart, just as night follows day. But you can see night slowly seep into day, especially when sleep has been scared away. I want to see it, but it's under the skin. In my blood. I don't understand it. I am its host and I can't see it or feel it. At least, not yet. Could you dye a cell and see it travel around? How would you track it? How would you know? Wish I had paid more attention at school. And it frustrates me and angers me. This thing is inside me and I can't get rid of it. There's only one way to kill it. Wash dark thoughts separately...

And within these random thoughts, I can't stop seeing them. Over and over and I can't stop seeing them. They're everywhere. The Disappeared. They are in my dreams. One in particular appears more than the others. That boy at uni who killed himself. Was he one of us? Us. I'm an 'us' now. Is there a membership card for that? I can't remember his name and I hate myself. I hate myself anyway. Will I become part of this ghost march? Is this punishment for not paying more attention back then?

And I hate that I'm not meant to tell people, you know, just in case. In case *they* turn the other cheek. In case they say, well… if you lie with dogs. In case they are pretending not to notice. In case they think I'm dirty.

Part of an exclusive club now. Am I sure? I'm positive! Gallows humour. Christ. I mean you have to, don't you? 'Cos if you didn't… Round it goes. Where it stops? Nobody knows! I wish it could be then now. Are they really sure? But this is no dream, this is really happening. They know. They told you already. It's there. And it's growing. Be patient. A patient.

Patient. Waiting.

They do know, you know—the doctors—what it looks like. They've been able to pinpoint it, under the microscope. You can see what it looks like too. I mean, if you wanted to. Of course I looked, I couldn't resist it. And you know what? It *is* a kinda green colour. Not serpentine, though. Marvels of modern science, huh? Watch out though! The floor is lava!

And down you fall.

Down the rabbit hole and through the looking glass.

The channel changed and now it's a medical drama. Keep up.

Endless waiting. Endless corridors. Is the end in sight? Of course not. There is no finish line. Not yet, anyway. Just appointments. More blood. Withdrawing and withdrawn. New terms. Levels see-sawing under the skin. In there. Still circling. No control. Injections of knowledge. Injections of humour. The four humours. Here comes bile.

Depressed, distressed, repressed. *Eat, Sleep, Rave, Repeat.* Stop the world I wanna get off.

Meanwhile, it grows. This not-so-snake-like intruder. Chasing its tail.

Meanwhile, I wait.

And over and over it goes. Round and round. My brain can't take this. My body can't take this. And still the withdrawals— from friends, from work, from life. Night after sleepless night— and the corner-of-the-eye terror, and endless corridors, and unknowingly I have lost the wrong kind of weight. I have perfected that haunted look. And still, somehow, the numbers aren't right. The levels are in the wrong place and the magic potions are not mixed and ready for you until you level up. But it isn't game over. So there is that. But I do feel like a lab rat in a trap. But it's better now. It will be. Medical advances. Suppression. I take one step forward. Maybe two back though. More like three. Try not to worry. And on it goes and years have passed and when you finally accept that it's time to start medication and steel yourself and quietly praise yourself for making this decision, you discover that the gods have spoken, the stars are aligned and the scales are tipped... now you are officially ill enough to qualify for life.

The orange one is twice a day. Twelve hours apart. Plus another, for good measure. Three Little Pills.

So this is it now. This is it. And those not-so-little pills are popped. And do you know what? They slay the serpent. Every day. Little by little. And now months have passed and it's no longer a great beast. It is practically invisible. It's still invincible though. That green glow may have evaporated, but it clings on. Hidden, yes, but no longer able to replicate. The battle's not won but the victory will be ours.

The Silent Alarm

Mark Carlisle

+

How can you ever explain colour,
the true beauty of an abstract art,
to someone who has never seen,
when you are, already, yourself,
caught up in a horrendous dream?

You are a quite adorable,
prickly, poisonous cactus
that everyone tries to avoid.
It could happen to any one of us,
if you were to believe all the noise.
Then even the tiniest little prick...

Don't touch me!
Don't touch me!
Don't touch me!

The invisible barrier is raised
as the silent alarm goes off,
subconsciously triggering
an incomprehensible world.

Continually, it is shrilling out
its deafening cacophony:
total damming silence,
this pure singularity.

A void of word
where nobody
dares speak.

How can you explain
the unexplainable
when you don't
understand it yourself?

Before long, you realise you are lost
in an onion soup of your thoughts.
Chasing the hatter down the rabbit hole
already knowing, deep down in your heart,
he is totally mad and cannot be caught.

Lost in the mirrored maze,
walled in by so many reflections,
trapped behind your own eyes,
softly wrapped up in cotton wool,
thinking it would be strange,
but it's actually quite normal.

Struggling to somehow awaken,
you search for a small glimmer of hope
or some faint trace of clarity.

But it seems everyone else is so busy
inserting themselves into the onion,
maybe somehow believing that
this dream is not just real,
it is just another
sad lonesome

soliloquy?

It's not and they are wrong!
Now you have to wake up.

Start by peeling away the onion
    layers.
Then this nightmare will have an end.
You are not your own worst enemy
when you are your own best friend.

The door of your prison is open.
Take it one step at a time.
First, you turn off the silent alarm
the second you release your mind.

Reducing HIV-related Stigma

Stigma continues to be the main barrier to better health outcomes for people living with HIV, preventing early diagnosis or resulting in discrimination. *Scotland's Anti-Stigma Strategy: Road Map to Zero* was launched by HIV Scotland in December 2017. It outlined the need for a holistic approach to actions designed to tackle HIV-related stigma. By defining HIV-related stigma, we can measure it and monitor the progress and effectiveness of our actions. Successfully tackling HIV-related stigma would allow us to increase testing opportunities to diagnose early, improve care for people living with HIV, prevent discrimination on the basis of someone's status and help us get to zero new infections.

Emergence See

Mark Carlisle

+

HIV was the catalyst
our antiretrovirals
have provided a key
now times of change
have come upon us
just like the caterpillar
all there is left to see
as you finally emerge
from your chrysalis is
which colour butterfly
are you hoping to be?

,

A Long Time

dedicated to Kevin Owen

James McAbraham

+

it's been a long time since
anyone touched me, or I touched them
as they touched each other

for them, you could see
the world was still fresh
a place where innocence still coloured their view
where sexuality, sensuality, lust and love
were a game where everyone won!

hands running through each other's hair
holding each other's face as they embrace
exuding—oblivious to their surroundings
with building passion, tension and desire
as their bodies
like the ebbing and flowing of the sea
moved with each other
the tides coming in
as the sea covers the sand
a neck bends and gives way

their kissing became intense
as searching eyes negotiated
their trust and hope in each other
in wonder of life's rhythm and beat

the intensity became too much
and searching for a cigarette
I recall how I used to love
and be loved—
and express with my body
what my soul and spirit knew

how it has all changed!

the last time someone touched me like that
was the day my world collapsed!
so early into a new relationship—
the day I learnt I was positive

even on that night
when I felt tarnished and dirty
he came to me and reminded me
I was for him still beautiful
and loved with tenderness and passion

the innocence of my world is no more
a place of tragedies and loss
of changes to follow not seen
even trust betrayed by another

again, I find myself fumbling for a cigarette
and wishing I too
could experience the intensity again—
when I am ready
I certainly will
and without shame, even
in the face of judgement!

for change and the past
inform the future
they don't have to dictate it

a war rages
in our bodies, in the world
freedom fighters in a united cause
fighting prejudice, ignorance, fear
regressive legislation, corporate greed
and government complacency
while around us our comrades
are ill, denied medications, dying!

yet, even in the noise of war
if you look and listen
the sea still dances with the sand
and our hearts
can be refilled with wonder

THE STAGE DOOR

Welcome to the Theatre of Awkward

Nathan Sparling

+

Waiting at the door
not yet open but
a gathering crowd
all waiting to enter
the Theatre of Awkward

For some, regular
first time for others
Everyone looking up, down
at their phones, anything—
no eye contact

The door opens
You take your number
Seated in rows
twiddling thumbs
the auditionees wait

Number Eight
Your time is now
projecting your name
to the eager audience
No privacy here

Then to stage right
lights on, curtain drawn
prick, poke and prod
with needles & swabs
your tests now done

The standing ovation
the stage door open,
walking free, duty done
PrEP in hand
sexual liberation to come

HIV Testing

Knowing your status is important so that you can access medication early, if needed, to ensure you can live a long and healthy life. Access to HIV testing in Scotland is free at sexual health clinics or through your GP, but the stigma surrounding testing or the fear of a diagnosis can sometimes be a big barrier. HIV Scotland carried out a detailed piece of work, *HIV Testing in Scotland*, that made 32 recommendations to health boards and the Scottish Government to scale up access to HIV testing, through better workforce development, easier access to clinics and promoting testing through a public campaign. 13% of people living with HIV in Scotland don't know they have it, so if you think you may have been at risk, get tested and know your status.

Message to My Younger Self

Rio

+

First: don't let the bastards grind you down. Believe in yourself.

Second: take control of your health as much as possible and be careful the doctors don't treat other conditions as side effects.

Third: enjoy the music you love, laughter and time with family and friends.

Fourth: you do have rights, find the best support.

Your family don't have to live like refugees. You are meant for this world. You and your children are children of the universe too... shine.

It will be a rough ride for you, motherhood. You will be told to abort by a GP in '89. You won't listen. You'll always want a family; it'll be the biggest wish of your life. You won't plan to be a single parent, but that is what will happen.

You will be refused surgery because the surgeon won't put his team at risk for the likes of you—his words.

Stigma will make you move twice already: once with a police escort, with babes in arms, because of a violent neighbour, and again to escape the damaging gossip. Stigma will make you hide away, be invisible.

Try to look at the situations that will happen to you and know it's not your fault. Bringing up kids is hard, but your kids will become kind, caring, fun and funny adults and will give you at least one very special grandchild. They will make you very proud and will teach you lots.

The children finding out will be tricky. You'll realise they need to know, to understand why their mother is some days unwell and often withdrawn. Your eldest will find out accidentally by reading a letter waiting to be posted. During the summer holidays, you will explain while you are raspberry picking with them and it will all seem fine. Then the shit will hit the fan. School will start again and your eldest will tell a friend. This will be something you arrange and agree by speaking to the child's mother, who you know and like and who lives nearby. All will be fine until another kid, a wee devilish one, gets the secret out of them and starts spreading it around. Your youngest will also find out and tell her teacher you have 'HMV'. We will laugh, but our world will change then.

Your children will be bullied, will have to fight their way out of situations. Neighbourhood kids will surround the house, shouting abuse. There will be no help. All this will impact your relationship with your children. You will feel guilty; they will be angry and upset. But you will all come through this in your own ways. The friends who stick by them will still be great friends many years later.

You will give what you can to your children: lots of camping, caravan, campers, youth hostels while they are young—even going to T in the Park and four foreign holidays. The pressure will be off when you are all off elsewhere. No judgements. The breaks away are when you will feel most connected to the world.

You will go to study shiatsu—a big love in your young life—and start reading Osho's books again. Shiatsu will give you an understanding of health and be good for your mental health. You will hold on to all you learn there. It will be three years well spent with understanding tutors, but you will never feel confident to disclose to the class.

HIV is part of you, part of who you are now. You will meet many lovely people who are also HIV and who have their own journeys. Also many lovely people who aren't!

Believe in the future. New effective meds are on the way with fewer side-effects. There is light at the end of the tunnel!

Things will get easier. The virus will be hard to live with, the stigma will be impossible sometimes and will affect your self-worth—but beating stigma and normalising HIV will be something you will help change.

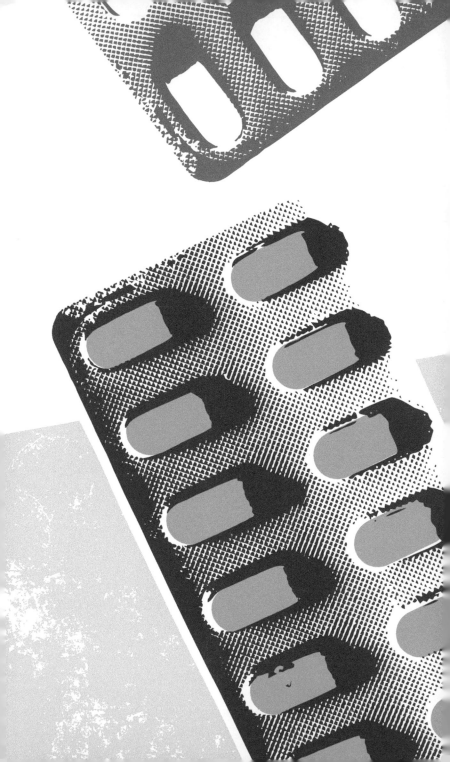

Will You be Able to Tell Us About Your Story?

Fraser Serle

+

Well, I can, but it will be redacted
The stigma many people living with HIV feel means they
    are not out about their status
I'm a bit in and out with my family about mine
Though I guess, maybe, after this, I'm gonna be fully out to
    them
That's if those I've not told care to read this; I'm not telling
    them I'm doing it
Why would I? I don't tell them all my other business
My immediate family knows
My sister guessed several years back
She'd seen my Facebook posts about training to be a peer
    mentor at Positively UK
We were both down in Brighton at the same time
So, we met up
I said, *I've something to tell you*
She was like, *Doh! I do read your posts*
None of the rest of the family had got it, though
I think it all got lost in between my posts of hot guys and
    Snoopy cartoons
As it was my business to share we agreed nothing would be
    said
Only last year, we were all going to Liverpool
I was like, *fuck, I'm going to have to say something*
My mental health had been a bit blurgh! Big time

So, I thought, *How do I do it?*

Since my diagnosis, I have been determined not to become my condition

So many people do; they let their health condition become their life

My HIV is only a wee part of me (sometimes not so wee)

Before meds, I never knew what my CD4 count or viral load were

I'd go for my check-up, get the results and promptly forget them when I left the clinic

I wrote them down a couple of times and was like, *wtf, what does it matter?*

Whose benefit is this for? I'm well

I'd been on meds since 2009

Had a few combos and they were quite easy to remember

Atripla, made me more bonkers than I already was

At work I was all *like I give fuck* when I was informed the CEO could lose their job due to the service failing to meet its DH target

My move to Truvada and Etravirine came when I mentioned the dream about babies being buried up to their heads, surrounded by snakes

Then with Eviplera I was down to one tablet a day

The move to Odefsey was harder

I couldn't remember the name

(I've just looked at my bottle to check the spelling)

When I started it was known by a series of letters

e/r/t/a I think

My way to tell my family (and remember the name)

was to post a link to an Odyssey track with a quip about the names being similar

When I arrived in Liverpool, everyone had gone to bed, except my sister

She said, *They know*

They all, of course, looked it up, thinking it was a mental-health treatment

I'd been in England for 28 years

When you live far away it is easier to hide stuff

Or be someone else, if you want or need to be
I'm always me
My mum is quite cool and enlightened
She'd been a volunteer with Positive Help and has
    demonstrated against Donald Trump
So I think hearing I'd deliberately not told her was hard
We chatted, and she asked questions
Not telling people you love is not easy
Now I feel a weight has been lifted
I can take my tablets openly
Talk about things that are happening and my experiences
    as a peer mentor
Hence now I'm at the stage of telling my story
Well, the redacted version anyway

Our First Breath is IN

James Stewart

+

IN comes the air
IN comes the oxygen
IN comes the dust
IN comes the world, the universe

giving us life

then OUT goes the breath

OUT goes the air
OUT goes the carbon
OUT goes ourselves, our thoughts and words

IN and OUT

I'm breathing
You're breathing
And the air, the world, the universe is getting IN

past the skin, through the defences, over the barrier
and IN

Is it clean?
Are you clean?
Are you dirty now?
Are you soiled?
Did you ever let something in you didn't want,
didn't even expect?

Why didn't you cover your mouth?
Why didn't you wear a mask?
You knew the risks!
What's the matter with you?!
Did you want to get infected?

I was having sex
as natural as breathing
I was having sex:
IN and OUT

Disclosure

A person's HIV status is private. It is your right to choose whether to tell someone (or 'disclose') that you have HIV. However, there are some situations where you are legally required to share your status. You don't have to tell a sexual partner that you have HIV, as long as you take appropriate precautions to prevent sexually transmitting HIV—such as becoming undetectable. When it comes to employment, HIV is irrelevant in most cases; however, in healthcare or military jobs there is a requirement to share your status with an employer. There is no legal requirement for you to share your HIV status before undergoing any type of medical examination or treatment, playing sports, or in education. You do have to disclose your status, when asked, to apply for insurance or an international-travel visa.

Texan Condoms

Kevin Crowe

+

.

2017

Yet another World AIDS Day service. Yet another day reflecting on all those whose lives had been cut short because of a virus no-one knew existed. While their bodies were being damaged by cancers and infections they had no way of resisting, they were being told they had brought it on themselves by their irresponsible behaviour. They were blamed for an excess of love. They were condemned as a danger to others.

Times have changed: the virus and its effects can now be treated. We can now love without being judged. We can marry. But as I sit next to my husband, my partner of over a quarter of a century, I am not immune from survivor guilt.

1979

The fierce Texan sun exacerbated my hangover.

I drank as much water as I could manage, attempting to ease the discomfort in my dehydrated body. I packed my sleeping bag and tent and headed south along Highway 87.

Wearing a hat and long-sleeved shirt to protect my pale features from the sun, I thought about the previous night's excesses. I had no recollection of how I'd got back to the campsite, but I do remember the wonderful evening of outlaw music, Lone Star beer and sensimilla weed—at least I was told it was sensi: it could just have been very strong grass.

I'd dumped my stuff at the camp site, then headed the few miles to Luckenbach, arriving there mid-afternoon. Sitting outside the bar drinking Lone Star and chewing on beef jerky, my accent attracted others, all wanting to know about me; none of them had ever met a Brit before and were amazed I'd found my way to this tiny hamlet in the middle of nowhere. One gnarled, weather-beaten redneck invited me on a rattlesnake hunt:

"We gas their nests. We only shoot 'em if we have to: shooting 'em destroys the skin, which means we can't sell it. We sell the venom to hospitals for snakebite serum and the body to restaurants. It's fun."

I politely declined.

Someone else asked, "Hey man, why not stay for the dance tonight?" He spoke in that low, lazy, sexy Texan drawl—each word seems to take a minute and each sentence an eternity. I looked up at this giant of a man, with long brown hair, unkempt beard and a t-shirt with "Cosmic Cowboy" on the front and "Willie Nelson for President" on the back.

I did stay for the dance: lots of loud country music from Waylon and Willie wannabes, Lone Star, Bourbon and weed. I made many friends, all of whose names I had forgotten by the morning. I do remember singing along to Willie Nelson's 'I Gotta Get Drunk' at the top of my voice.

Already the sun was creating a heat haze in the distance and, despite the hat and long sleeves, I could feel my skin beginning to burn. I took another long swig of water and stuck my thumb out at a passing car. It pulled up, the driver wound his window down and asked, "Where you headed, son?"

"San Antonio."

"You're in luck. Dump your stuff in the back."

The first thing I noticed was how cool the car was inside. Although I'd been travelling round the States for a while now, I hadn't got used to air conditioning. On this occasion, after the oppressive heat of the Texas summer, I was glad of the coolness.

I'd always had this image of Americans—and particularly

Texans—driving large gas-guzzling cars at high speed. The gas guzzling bit was probably still correct, judging by the size of the car (which he told me was a Buick), but President Carter had recently introduced a national 55 mph speed limit, and it was strictly enforced. So we cruised along at a much more sedate speed than I had expected from the other side of the pond, while the radio played Texan country.

"Well, son, what brings a Brit all the way to Texas?" Another low, lazy Texan drawl.

"I'm just spending a few months travelling round America, mainly in the south. Ever since I was a boy I've wanted to come to Texas. Ever since watching John Wayne films. And I love the music: Waylon, Willie, Guy Clark, Bob Wills—could listen to it all day."

"Wow, man, didn't know our music was popular over there! Good to know."

"Oh yes, it's really popular. There are country music festivals and lots of clubs."

I looked at the driver. A smile was playing across his face. "And what do you think now you're here?"

"Well, Texas is certainly big. And I wasn't expecting all this," I waved at the lush Hill Country scenery. "I didn't realise there was all this greenery. I love the sight of those hills covered in blue flowers."

"Yeah, it's beautiful, but you have to be careful where you put your feet."

I nodded. I told him about a walk I'd taken near a stream, and how much I was enjoying it until I saw a rattlesnake blocking the path. "I very carefully and very very slowly backed away and returned to the road."

He laughed. "A wise move." Without taking his eyes off the road, he stuck out his hand.

"I'm Hank." I shook his hand and told him my name was Sean, adding, "A good old Irish name, though I wasn't born there."

"Nice to meet you, Sean." After a short silence while I looked at the passing scenery, he asked, "So what's been your favourite bits of Texas so far?"

"Oh, Austin was special, particularly the World Armadillo

Headquarters. And yesterday I was at Luckenbach—truly memorable, except I can't remember much thanks to all the beer."

Hank guffawed. "Yeah, I've spent time at Luckenbach. I bet it wasn't just beer." At that moment, the Waylon Jennings song about the hamlet came over the airwaves. We both sang along to the radio. As the song faded out, we were both grinning.

"That was good," I said.

He nodded. "Sure was." He turned to me, taking his eyes off the road just for a moment, and asked: "Hey, back home do you have a girlfriend?"

"Nothing special," I replied.

"Hey, I would have thought a good lookin' dude like you would have had the girls running after him."

I laughed. "Me? Good looking? You must be joking!"

"Not at all. I really do think you're good lookin'."

"Yeah, well the girls don't think so. Not that I'm bothered. To tell you the truth, it's a bit of a relief."

"Now, why would that be?"

I just shrugged my shoulders. I wasn't about to say anything else; it was still illegal in Texas.

I felt his hand rest on my knee and gradually move to my thigh. I could feel myself getting aroused. "I reckon I know why you ain't interested in girls." He moved his hand back to the steering wheel.

"What are your plans when we get to San Antonio?" he asked.

"I don't really know," I replied. "Look for a campsite or cheap motel for a couple of nights, then head out west."

"Stop at my place for a while, if you like."

I wasn't sure. I was excited by the thought of spending time with a real Texan, perhaps even a cowboy or a rodeo rider. But there were so many stories of people being picked up and then hurt or even murdered. I knew nothing about Hank. Even his name could have been false, but he knew nothing about me either and I felt nauseous with desire.

Such was my reverie, I didn't notice that buildings had replaced the countryside, until we pulled up outside a condominium block.

"Here we are," Hank said. "Home—at least my home." I followed him along the manicured lawn and past the flower beds to his apartment, though 'apartment' didn't do justice to its opulence. Oil paintings on some walls, bookshelves on others, a crimson carpet with piles so thick you could lose yourself, a state-of-the-art hi-fi system, leather sofas and off to the side a kitchenette. Everything was spotless and in its place. Until he put on some music, the only sound was the humming of the air conditioning.

"Wow!" I said pirouetting around. "Wow! This is—well—just wonderful."

"Glad you like it. But I ain't no realtor—I didn't bring you here to sell you the place." He bent his index finger in the universal sign for 'follow me'. Sitting next to him in the car, I hadn't realised just how big he was: over six feet with bulging muscles covering his arms and upper body, he towered over my five feet five, pale and weedy body.

I followed him into the bedroom, which was even more opulent than the lounge. There were mirrors on the walls and on the ceiling above the large emperor-sized bed. From a fridge in the corner he produced a bottle of bourbon and filled two glasses, passing one to me. I took a sip of the smoky liquid, my hand shaking as I lifted the glass to my mouth.

"Nervous?" he asked.

My heart was racing, but I managed to shake my head. "No, just—just..." He ended my struggle for the right words by kissing me, deep and long. I felt so puny compared to him and wondered what it was about me that attracted him.

We made love, exploring every crevice of each other's bodies. Afterwards, we collapsed, breathless and sweating, arms around each other.

I must have dozed off, because the next thing I remembered was Hank kissing me and passing me another bourbon. "That was wonderful," he said.

"Yeah," I grinned, slightly embarrassed. I took a sip of the drink, then said, "Hope you don't mind me asking, but why did you use a condom? I mean, you can't get me pregnant."

"They don't just stop pregnancy." He was silent for a

moment, then continued: "Recently there's been an increase in fags getting Hep B." I must have looked puzzled. "Hepatitis B: it's a liver disease, and it can be spread by sex. A lot of people don't know anything about it, or how to protect themselves until it's too late." He hesitated, then continued, "I ain't saying you've got it, and I ain't saying I've got it. It's just a precaution. You don't mind, do you?"

I giggled. "If you can fuck like that, you can wear a whole boxful."

He grabbed me, and we made love again.

I stopped with him for four weeks. He showed me around San Antonio: the wonderful river walk, the Alamo, the restaurants (where I developed a taste for tacos and enchiladas), the art galleries, the night life. One night he took me to a gay club (though, being Texas, it couldn't be advertised as such), where he introduced me to lots of people.

Everyone referred to him as Rubber Man and there was some good-natured banter at his expense. One guy told me he'd take me back home with him, so I could experience real Texan sodomy: skin against skin. I declined; I was perfectly content with Hank.

Eventually, the time came when I had to leave. Before returning across the pond, I wanted to spend time in the desert and the Sierras. I'd stopped with Hank so long, I'd already decided not to bother with the Castro area of San Francisco. After all, what could I find there that Hank couldn't—hadn't—given me? Hank agreed it was probably time for me to leave; he was a freelance journalist and he'd just got a commission for a job that would take him to Louisiana for some research. There were tears when we parted. He headed east; I went west.

1989

Benjamin had come home to die. He had insisted. He had told the doctors he wanted to spend his last days in familiar and friendly surroundings. His treatment had come too late and the side effects were so bad they had taken him off the drugs. He had lost so much weight, we could see his bones and he lacked the strength to walk unaided. His body was covered in cancerous lesions, some looking like small red boils, others with the appearance of those large, purple bruises we sometimes get when we bash a hand against a hard surface. He was incontinent. Because of his oral herpes, he couldn't chew food and could only swallow with difficulty. His carers—of which I was one—were continually wiping his dripping mouth, cleaning him, changing his incontinence pads and moving him to avoid bed sores.

We also rolled his joints. Cannabis was one of the few things that could relieve some of the pain. It also helped him sleep and stimulated his appetite. We would sit him up, liquidise his food and patiently feed him with teaspoons—small enough quantities for him to swallow.

He'd had several bouts of pneumonia and, eventually, when his immune system was no longer capable of resisting anything, one final attack led to his death. Just another AIDS statistic.

I remember the conversation we had when, just three years earlier—following some illnesses—he tested positive for HIV antibodies, and he was told he had developed AIDS.

We went out for a drink, spoke about this and that, neither of us seeming to want to mention the doctor's verdict. Part way through his third pint he looked at me, smiling sadly.

"I think I know when I got this thing, I really do." He took another swig of his beer. "I believe it was the summer of 1979, before anyone even knew about AIDS. After I'd finished at university, I spent a couple of months in San Francisco, stopping in Castro. Christ, I was like a kid in a sweet shop! The bars, the bathhouses, the steam rooms, the saunas. More available men than I could handle in a lifetime of cruising, and whatever you were into—no matter how weird—it was available." He was silent for a few moments, then said: "At least I had fun, I suppose."

He finished his pint. "I think I'd like to go home now."

2017

As the final hymn begins, I take my husband's hand, aware that

Benjamin would never know what that felt like. A life-long gay activist and a secular Jew who had withstood both anti-Semitic and homophobic violence, like Moses he never saw the liberation he did so much to make possible. As we shuffle out of the church and fasten our coats against the cold winter wind, I hear Benjamin telling me the best way to remember him is to live our lives to the full and celebrate our love.

PrEP

Pre-Exposure Prophylaxis (PrEP) is a pill that people who are HIV-negative can take to stop them acquiring HIV. In 2017, Scotland became the first country in the UK to offer PrEP on the NHS to those who need it thanks to the PrEP for Scotland campaign that was led by HIV Scotland. PrEP can work for anyone at high-risk of acquiring HIV through sex, but more work is required to ensure PrEP reaches everyone that needs it, including people who inject drugs, trans and non-binary people and women.

What is a Man if Not an Anchor?

Nobody

+

burdened by the weight of fear
I wander the road backwards trying to veer
into the right, into the light
without falling forwards or still without life

without sight I could wander
forever unconscious
making choices I'd wonder
if I'm proud to believe

proud to feel pride in a place once again
a life without love might just be in vain
or even the same as that one small breath
working up courage, working up strength
grounded by nothing and built to be free
transcendent, translucent, the start of the story

preserved by the strain of time
the crown to hold, the crown could be mine
crystal clear in the depths of the night
the road that I'm walking is bathed in moonlight
moments will come that test our strength
challenge our reasons for being
the reasons I know deep down in my soul
the reasons to live and to love over all

Access to Medication

Because treatment is part of the prevention toolkit, access to effective medication is extremely important. In Scotland, we adopt the test-and-treat model where treatment is offered almost immediately after diagnosis. This provides better health outcomes for people living with HIV, as they can manage the condition better before the immune system becomes too damaged. New medicines are being developed all the time which support long-term adherence, have fewer side effects, or are less resistant. Maintaining access to good-quality medication is vital to improving and maintaining a good quality of life for people living with HIV, whilst preventing onward transmission.

Untitled

Matthew Lynch

+

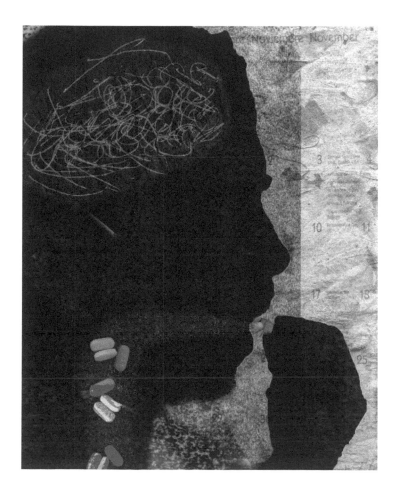

Víreas

J. William James

+

I was ten when Sister Orla got sick. At first it was fever, and we all thought it would pass. Then came vomiting and dysentery. She grew thinner and weaker. The nuns didn't have a name for the disease back then. Even Sister Shannon, who had studied medicine in the capital, didn't know what it was.

Mother Superior decided that Orla had to be hidden from the pilgrims. If word got out there was sickness on the island, people would stop coming to commune with the nuns. The convent's income would dry up, and we'd all go hungry. So Orla was locked away in a basement room. I was angry about that for a long time.

Sister Cara volunteered to take care of her. Mother Superior gave me permission to help—it was too big a job for one person. I was pleased to be with them together, even if sometimes it was unpleasant work. Cara and Orla got on famously; Cara could always say the right thing to make Orla laugh.

Orla started having terrible night sweats. She said it was like waking in a flooded grave. Every morning, I would strip her bed and remake it with clean linen while Cara bathed her in a copper bathtub. Then I would fetch her breakfast: it had to be soup because her throat was too swollen to eat solids. Shannon prescribed garlic, turmeric and goat's thorn for the infection. It was hard to say if they worked—if ever the swelling died down it would soon return. I felt a kind of guilt when I ate fish or bread; I was enjoying something Orla couldn't.

When she was well enough, Orla spent her time sewing. She embroidered patterns on cloth in fine-coloured thread. She taught me how. When I had finished my chores, we'd sit together and sew, often in silent concentration. She spent weeks working on one design: in white and grey she stitched three long, thin spires emerging from a sea of black and blue. She said she had seen it in a dream: "They were narwhals. They erupted from the ocean with their tusks aligned, like an ivory trident thrust into the sky, or a candelabrum of bone. They were a pod of gods. They were pointing the way to heaven."

I asked Sister Nuala what dreams were. We were in the garden weeding flower beds. "Dreams are our minds playing tricks while we sleep," Nuala explained, without looking up from the lavender bush she was attending. "It's silly to think too much about them." I told her that Orla seemed to think they were something more. "Sister Orla is sick. Sick people think silly things."

We were silent for a long while before I spoke again. "Can animals be gods?"

Nuala put down her trowel and turned to me. "Is Orla filling your head with nonsense again? There are no gods. Animal or otherwise. Only goddesses."

+

One afternoon, I was on the beach collecting pebbles. I wanted to make a sculpture out of them, for Orla. A man appeared on the sands. It was unusual to see a pilgrim so far from their lodgings on the other side of the island. He seemed drunk, stumbling over himself as he came towards me.

"Do you live here, boy?"

I tried to ignore him. Mother Superior had forbidden me from talking to the pilgrims. I wanted him to leave me alone.

"Is one of those whores your mother? Answer me, boy."

He seethed with drunken anger. He must have been rejected by the nuns; they would not commune with the likes of him. Before he got any closer, I turned and ran back to the convent, leaving my bucket of pebbles behind.

When I got back, panting but safe, there was no-one about. The door to the library was closed; the nuns were having a meeting. Curious, I pressed my ear to the door. I heard Shannon's voice, "One of the pilgrims must have given it to her when they communed. There is no other explanation."

"No good man would inflict so evil a curse."

"Not knowingly, no."

"Whoever it was, he will be long gone by now."

"Who is to say he is the only one who carries it? There could be others."

There was a silence.

"You realise, sisters, that this changes everything."

The gravity in their voices scared me.

+

Mother Superior decided that all men were to leave the island. I was glad. Shannon said it was to keep the sisters safe from the *víreas*. That was a new word we all learned—*víreas*. A new devil to fear. "But *how* did they give it to Orla?" I would ask.

The nuns each gave the same reply, "You will learn when you're older." The details of the goddess's communion were not for a young boy to know.

Orla was finally free to leave her room. She asked to see the sea, but she was too weak to walk. Sister Imani, ever ingenious, made a wheelchair. I pushed Orla along the track away from the convent and up the hill to the windharp. The sky was clear, and you could see the mainland in the distance. Gulls were soaring on the wind and the harp was playing its beautiful, peculiar song. We sat together, small before the immensity of the ocean. I told her the view reminded me of her embroidery. "We just have to wait for the narwhals to come." She smiled, and gazing across the water she said, "They'll come." Her voice croaked, each word difficult because of her swollen throat. "I know the gods will guide me."

"You must hate him," I said, after a time.

"Who?"

"The man who made you sick."

49

"No, I have forgiven him. I know he didn't mean to. He must be sick too. He will be as scared as I am."

+

With no pilgrims, and therefore no communions, the convent's income disappeared. Savings had to be made. "We shan't be buying fish any longer," Mother Superior explained one lunchtime, "We will have to be austere. These are trying times."

Nuala smirked and said, "We'd have more to go round if there wasn't deadweight to feed."

With that, Cara tore out of her seat and fled the dining hall in tears. None of the other nuns made a move. I asked to be excused and went after her. I found her in the garden, strewn on the lawn. I didn't know what was wrong. I had never seen her cry before.

"How can they be so heartless?" she sobbed. "She isn't dead yet. They've been talking like she's already dead."

The reality thumped me then and there. That was when I first realised Orla was going to die. I fell beside Cara, keening like a banshee.

+

Orla's funeral was held on the hill by the convent. We wore white, the colour of life beyond death. Under my robe, hidden, I wore Orla's narwhals embroidered across my chest. As her body was burned, Mother Superior spoke twenty seven prayers—one for each of her years alive. I held Cara's hand as she silently wept. The harp played a mournful song, as though the wind understood our loss. I didn't look at the pyre. I looked out over the sea to the sky. I knew that's where she was. I knew the gods would guide her.

Undetectable = Untransmittable

A fundamental question people living with HIV have is, *Will I pass on HIV to my sexual partner?* The science is now very clear. Someone living with HIV who is taking effective medication as prescribed, and therefore has reduced the level of the virus in the body to a level where it is undetectable, will not pass HIV on to their sexual partners. This is known as 'Treatment as Prevention'. The 'Undetectable = Untransmittable' message reduces the shame and fear faced by people living with HIV; they can't pass the virus on. It also encourages access to treatment at an early stage, therefore providing better health outcomes for people living with HIV.

afterwards

atop the bedsheets

RJ Arkhipov

+

afterwards   i trace the edges of you
words bead   impatient
glistering upon the pale page of your skin
words   absent of tense
find themselves in my caress   bristling
words   pregnant of a moment

with each of these encounters
i press a scar i have not known
the brine musk of spent love
salting a wound that runs deep

and the moment is transformed
a toused bed sheet   becomes a shroud
the gentle precussion of our heart beats
scoring   a funeral march for men we did not know
our gutteral sighs   sorrowful wails   howling

were we, like our encounters, unprotected?

It Couldn't be Me

Michael Nugent

+

I will never forget that day—July 4th, 2016. The day I received my little silver package in the post. Little did I know just how important a package I had just received. It was my BioSURE HIV Self Test kit. That was the day I discovered I was HIV positive and a day that changed my life completely.

I mind opening the package and being excited to use the kit; it just looked so simple to use, and the fact that I would get almost instant results made me excited. I was naïve, thinking I could tick it off my list. I could never contract the virus... because I was always safe.

The feeling of excitement didn't last too long, as I opened the package and followed the three simple steps... prick my finger, suck up some blood into the test valve and then poke it into the activator tube. Fifteen minutes and the results would show... well, I almost followed the instructions step-by-step, but instead of laying my sample upright and letting the liquid slowly saturate, I placed it flat, and in that instant, I saw my blood flood the tube and instantly *two* solid lines appeared.

Grabbing the instructions, I searched for a warning or caution not to place it flat as it would invalidate the results, but instead all I could read was that the results were 99.7% accurate. *Fuck me.* I thought I would have a higher chance of winning the lottery than catching HIV.

I wanted to throw the test in the bin and pretend it never happened. It was wrong, it had to be! But my brain kicked into auto-mode—don't know if this was with the shock, horror, fear and disbelief of being HIV positive—and before I knew it, I was standing in my GP crying to see a doctor. I mind saying to the receptionist, "I have to see the doctor. I have just done an HIV test, and it's come back positive."

She replied, "You'll have to make an appointment."

To which all I could hear myself saying was, "I need to see a doctor now. Otherwise when I leave here I am going to put myself under a train." I broke down in floods of tears.

In that instant she realised what I said and got me the doctor. Walking into the room, all I could do was wave this silver package around, unable to speak with the tears running down my face! "Please tell me this is wrong."

To my shock he replied, "I didn't know you could do home testing for HIV," as he opened a website to check the credentials and quickly closed it when he'd seen the test was certified. He then said, "I've never diagnosed anyone with HIV, although there are patients within this practice who are positive." Followed by, "This reminds me of the time in EastEnders when Mark was diagnosed."

I mind the words being said clearly, and all I could think was, "Wait a fucking minute here, doc. This is my life, I'm not a fucking fictional character." I just wanted to walk out the room there and then, but I needed help. I needed to be tested to prove the test was wrong, and he knew that too.

As the nurse wasn't in, it was going to take at least two more days before he could even take my bloods, then I would have to wait for the results. Knowing that I could not wait that long and had to know, he referred me to the Sandyford Clinic, a sexual health service in Glasgow City. I asked him to dispose of the test. I couldn't bear to carry it anymore, and whilst I was leaving the room his last words to me where, "I hope you are in the 1%, otherwise that's just shite!" *Yeah, no shit there Sherlock!*

I attended the clinic that night and had to return two days later for results.

The morning of my results came. I was due to go into the

Sandyford in the afternoon, but I had a feeling that everything was going to be okay and I had made a mistake with the test, but that feeling soon went. I went into the shower to get ready. As soon as I stood under the water, I collapsed against the wall with more tears than the shower itself, and my brain felt numb. I was planning on going in alone, but I couldn't and called my sister to take me in.

On the journey there, we just kept saying to each other that it was going to be okay, we were going to come back out laughing. When we arrived, we weren't waiting long when this man came out and called my name. As we walked over, my sister just a few steps behind me, the guy looked at me and said, "Are you sure you want her to come with you?"

"Of course I am. She's my sister," I replied. But in that instant, I knew that I was not going to hear good news. My stomach was churning, and my mind was blank. We walked into the consultation room and before I could even sit down on the seat, I heard the man say, "We have your result back, and it is positive."

I collapsed, bursting into tears with my head clasped between my hands. Then I heard my sister say, "Aww, son," as she too burst into tears.

I was then advised that an appointment would be arranged with my specialist doctor within the next couple of weeks, handed some leaflets and left to go my merry way home.

The following few weeks were a rollercoaster ride of a journey. The first thing I did when I got home was go out and visit all my family and close friends; I was terrified that I could have infected someone else. Each time I was expecting to be kicked to the kerb and disowned. After all, who wants to know or be around someone with who is HIV positive? To my shock, time and time again, I received love, comfort and words of strength and was told to stay strong, even though none of us really knew what the situation was! And I am sure, just like me, we all thought the worst.

The following days I began educating myself about HIV (Don't use Google. It will terrify you with the misinformation and scary stories out there!) and finding out about all its mechanics. In this time, I discovered the magical word 'undetectable'. Something I had never before heard.

Over these weeks, I had to visit my specialist to have bloods taken and check my heath. I was in a very lucky place, as I found out that my body was dealing with the virus well. I had a high CD4 count (a healthy immune system) and a very low viral load (level of HIV within my blood). Even though I had a low viral load, it was still detectable, so for the safety of everyone around my and also for my own health, I choose to begin treatment. But one thing I was assured was that I should have an undetectable viral load within a few weeks.

Over the next few weeks I took my tablet religiously at the same time every day. Although I knew that I had a low viral load and therefore was non-infectious, and by taking the ARVs I was ensuring that I would not be able to become infectious, I still found myself keeping an arms' distance from people. Deep down I still knew I was HIV positive.

Finally, the day of my results came; it was the day I was going to find out if I has become undetectable. I am not going to lie, inside I was terrified. I remember being in the room and asked by the doctor, "What would you like to know?" And before he could finish his sentence, I responded, "My viral load". There up on his screen he brought up my results, and his words echoed in my mind, "You have a non-detectable viral load."

I saw the words "RNA NON-DETECTED". I mind staring it that screen for what seemed an eternity, then telling the doc, "I want a copy a that." Once I had a copy of the results in my hand, it was like my life was given back to me there and then!

I took the results straight home to my sister. I mind showing her the paper and seeing that glint come back in her eye, as then we both knew for sure that everything was going to be okay. I can and will live a long and healthy life.

That night for the first time in many weeks, I found myself rolling around the carpet playing wrestling with my nephews and niece, something that I had been longing to do but had been too scared to before.

Since that moment, I have taken ownership of my diagnosis. I have been open about my status, and through that I have learned a lot of lessons and misperceptions along the way. Now I use my experience and gained knowledge to educate others on today's facts and raise awareness around HIV and sexual health.

I have taken the rubble that once was and rebuilt a bright future ahead. I work closely with the sexual-health organisation Terrence Higgins Trust as both a volunteer and a positive-voices speaker—we attend schools, workplaces and organisations, talking openly about our lived experiences and telling our stories. I work with HIV Scotland as both a positive-person advocate and as support for the National Involvement Network, who ensure people living with HIV/AIDS (PLWH) are receiving the support they need and that their voices are being heard. I have become a peer-support mentor for PLWH and supported campaign groups like Youth Stop AIDS. I was featured in a documentary, *The Truth About HIV*, and have appeared on live-television broadcasts as well as in multiple national and local media talking about my diagnosis and the journey it took me on.

I have learned that people are not afraid of HIV; they are afraid because of the lack of education and awareness they have around HIV. As they say: it's not the HIV that kills me; it is the fear and stigma which does.

As people learn new facts about HIV, their perception of HIV changes, and, even more importantly, another person is hopefully saved from becoming HIV positive.

But for now, I am getting back to the old life I once had and loved, rebuilding my career and social life, and looking forward to making many more memories of my own with many happy years ahead.

Education

Schools have a duty to promote young people's rights to health and well-being and prepare young people's transition into adulthood. Unfortunately, access to sexual-health education is patchy, and in Scotland, on average, two young people are diagnosed with HIV every month. Relationships, Sexual Health, and Parenthood (RSHP) lessons should be where misconceptions about HIV and sexual health are addressed, but we know from research conducted by HIV Scotland that 34% of young people do not know how to minimise the risk of HIV, and 27% believe that HIV can be passed on from kissing. Significant work is required to ensure all young people receive up-to-date and accurate information about sexual health and HIV.

Uncertain, Learning, Unknown

Oliver

+

Taking the dive into the dating pool,

I felt so fucking clueless.

Trans. Gay. A child of the generation affected by Section 28.

I knew sexual health was important, despite not being taught it.

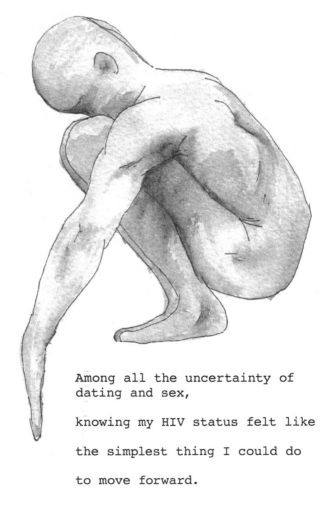

Among all the uncertainty of dating and sex,

knowing my HIV status felt like

the simplest thing I could do

to move forward.

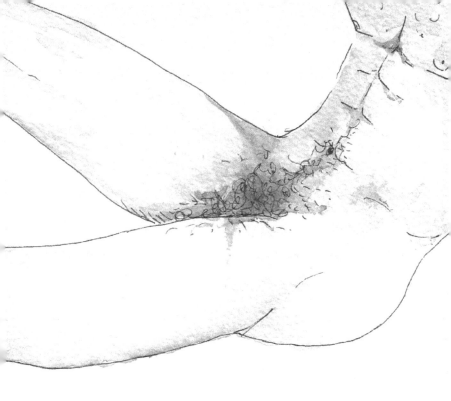

I felt very anxious about the prospect of
dating again after I came out. I remember
watching a particularly amusing and useful
BBC Three video on YouTube called 'Things Not
to Say to Someone Who's HIV Positive'.

As I was realising that statistically, in
the demographic of people I was going to be
dating, it was likely I'd meet someone living
with HIV at some point - and they might
choose to disclose their status to me - and
I'd not been in that position before.

Just as I didn't want anyone to react badly
when I disclosed my trans status, I felt it
was important to educate myself and be ready
if someone disclosed their HIV status to me.

PrEP comes up quite often on the dating scene. Apps like Grindr actually give an option to say if you're taking PrEP or not, and allow you to indicate your HIV status.

I've been offered PrEP already, and know if I was having sex I'd seriously consider it. I would have to consider if it interacts with other medication I'm on, and weigh that up against just saying safe via other means.

I've always been interested in scientific advances - I read a science degree at uni - and I remember the joy and delight I felt reading about the PARTNER studies a few years ago. Even before I identified as a gay man, knowing HIV could be reduced to an undetectable viral load and not be passed on at all was incredible. A true scientific advancement that saves lives.

It's shaped my feelings around dating people with HIV has a gay man now - HIV isn't something to be fearful of. I feel PrEP gives me the power to date freely without worrying about HIV transmission. I can be a part of the solution.

I'm still intimidated by all the naked torsos on Grindr though. It might be a while before that changes...

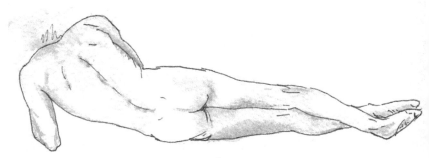

As a trans guy, finding adequate and appropriate sexual-health resources can be kind of tough, and sometimes the information I need doesn't even exist. (Even while researching to make this, I uncovered confusing and incorrect information from leading HIV charities.) Trans people are in one of the higher HIV-risk categories. So many are uncomfortable getting tested at all. Thankfully, HIV testing is pretty easy for me as it doesn't require access to any body parts I don't feel comfortable with.

Access to healthcare is currently pretty poor for trans people, and sexual health is no exception. I was surprised when one gay men's clinic said I was the first openly trans man to visit. But, I was the first person to ask at every place I went.

It made me wonder where everyone else goes to get tested. Asking around, I found that pretty much all of my friends don't go. Some rely on their partners to get tested, so only by proxy do they know they're STI-free too. Others just didn't know.

I've been asked (having explained I'm a trans man who's had no appointments yet at a gender clinic) whether I wear condoms. At another clinic, I had someone continually ask if I was sure a regular condom wouldn't fit my body. I ended up having to point at a blood-test tube to give a size guide and explain: "No, I am very sure even your smallest wouldn't fit me." I left, shocked that she clearly hadn't ever seen a trans guy's junk before. (There's actually no product on the market currently that would fit most trans men's genitalia. There should be - some men can penetrate.)

I found it hard to repeatedly come up against these barriers. We're left without sufficient

care so often that most of us end up
activists in one way or another, pushing for
better, for basics.

Talking about this in a public meeting, I
lobbied the NHS to set up a trans-specific
sexual-health centre in Scotland - which
would be the first and only one. Now there
is one, but sometimes the staff are still
unaware of basics about the anatomy of
trans people. There's such a wide variety in
terms of potential body parts and genital
configurations that it takes quite a sensitive
discussion to find out what each individual
needs in terms of sexual health. It's not
impossible, or even that hard - one day I
hope it'll be commonplace and easy to access
clinics where this sort of care is provided.

Looking into the research around trans
masculine sexual health, I wasn't particularly
surprised to find very little. There was one
literature review I found which discussed
exactly what research was missing and needed,
commenting that most studies focussed on
trans women, sex workers, and HIV. There was
almost nothing about trans men, or sexual
behaviour in general. Even academia didn't
know how to help. There was genuinely no
knowledge out there of how trans men can
have safe sex. It explained why I was finding
it hard to get solid advice or education
anywhere about how specifically I, as a trans
man, could maintain safety if I wanted to be
sexually active.

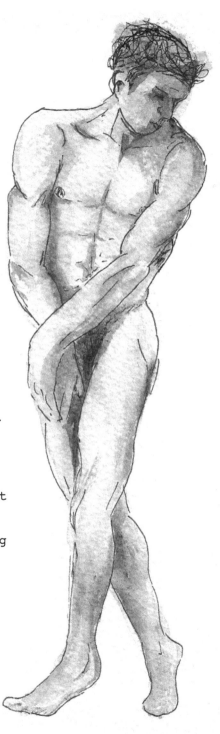

I learned all this
within the first year
of my transition.

I am painfully aware
that there's so much
missing, so little out
there.

Hopefully, by speaking
out, I can help it be
different someday.

Play it Again, SAM

Stephen Duffy

+

Vulgarity is in my blood. Unfortunately, so is HIV. The former has always loudly manifested itself at every feasible opportunity, usually in a stream of saucy double entendre. Mercifully, the same cannot be said for my HIV. Now please don't confuse this with gallows humour. Despite having lost a great many friends over the years to HIV, I do not equate it with death. And indeed these days, why would I? HIV is not something I intend to die from; it is instead a piss-poor, anarchic, incontinent and wholly unwelcome houseguest whom I have to live with for the rest of my days. However, I have always looked at the world through a haze of British seaside vulgarity and jokes about bum sex. For example, "That Mike Tyson, bet he's good with his fists in the ring." I promise I'll keep those to a minimum. But I steadfastly refuse to do anything else except laugh at the squelchy-squirty nature of our bodies and what we do with them for fun. (Believe me, if you're not smiling, you're doing it wrong.) I am now a 47-year-old man with a black-belt in advanced homosexuality and a vocation for sexual-health education, and I have no intention of changing. I make no apologies to anyone who might be offended by lewd and suggestive references to sex acts. As I like to tell the shocked wee faces of some of the school groups I talk to—"Your parents liked it bareback."

See, I knew I was gay before I knew it was different. I knew I was different before people told me it was wrong. And by people I mean the Catholic Church. I was born in 1971 and grew up in an age of unquestioned deference to the priesthood, an age before the many shocking revelations of abuse. I grew up in a new community near Glasgow, and my parish priest was an elderly Irishman with the look of an embittered civil servant who smelled of incense and Whyte & Mackay. He was the kind of bad priest who would ultimately turn into Father Jack Hackett. (For those who have never seen the TV sitcom *Father Ted*, Father Hackett is a rambling, violent, incoherent and sexually repressed alcoholic.) In retrospect there was nothing remotely hearty about the Cannon. 'Suffer little children' was his motto, and indeed many a classmate would emerge from confession in tears having been told how shameful they were.

The Cannon was the first adult I chose to confide in about my sexuality. In my mid-to-late teens I did readings at Mass and led the choir, and I was a genuinely devout young man, so I thought I'd be given a sympathetic hearing at confession. And indeed I was; a few Our Fathers, a few Hail Mary's and a promise to try and quell those thoughts and not act upon them. I minced out of church feeling I'd done the right thing. I probably had a wank to celebrate. But at Mass the following Sunday, the Cannon delivered a sermon, in which he singled out the late Rock Hudson and Liberace as examples of those who led deviant and promiscuous lives and how AIDS was God's judgement upon them, and all who contracted AIDS were the same. What strength got me to my feet at the front of the choir and walk out of the church I'll never know. Outside in the sunshine I cried for a solid half hour until the end of mass, and, as the congregation departed, I walked around to the rear of the church and knocked loudly upon the chapel-house door, which was opened by the elderly housekeeper. Red in the face and out of breath, I asked to see the Cannon. I wasn't invited in to wait. The door was closed in my face and I stood on the doorstep for what felt like an eternity until I heard the priest's footsteps, and he opened the door. I asked him what kind of God would send AIDS, send a plague to those whose only sin was to go to bed with someone they liked? He looked at me with blank, soulless expression. I turned around, called him a cunt, and never went back.

Later that year, I left school and became a tall, gangly, arty, sexually curious, post-Catholic, hopelessly middle-class and utterly naïve student in his first year at university, soaking up culture like a tall, gangly, arty, sexually curious, hopelessly middle-class and utterly naïve sponge. Naïve I certainly was, but I was, however, astute enough to realise that pubs and clubs weren't really my thing (that would change somewhat in my 30s) but I desperately wanted to meet other gay people, and I wanted to prove to myself that the Cannon words were indeed wrong. AIDS was scary. But I knew that, so I applied to volunteer with Scottish AIDS Monitor, then Scotland's leading HIV charity, and it welcomed me with open and eager arms. As much as I owe to university and to the traditional apprenticeship I served as a musician, it was SAM that turned out to be the making of me.

In SAM's Glasgow office, which was located in the basement of a grand Georgian terrace bordering Kelvingrove Park, I found myself in the company of the sort of people I imagined only ever lived in the pages of Armistead Maupin novels or on gritty Channel 4 documentaries. I met charming and funny street prostitutes (male, female and trans) and erudite, educated injecting drug users who dispelled every media stereotype. I met fabulous, fruity and filthy cropped-haired lesbians who taught me about Sylvia Plath and the joys of fisting. I met shy and retiring haemophiliacs who were also wide-eyed, cocaine-fuelled party animals. There was the most variegated and diverse group of gay men I've ever encountered. Lewis Carroll couldn't have come up with a more colourful cast. It was amazing, and I loved it. I loved going into the office. I loved the vague smell of damp from some of the training rooms. I loved the peeling magnolia paint in the reception area that just about covered several layers of hideous wall-chip. I loved the enormous cupboard stacked from top to bottom with condoms. But most of all I loved the people: the staff, the clients, my fellow volunteers, and the extraordinary lessons they taught me about living.

Those lessons were always enjoyable except when, quite early on, some of those people began to die. I was unprepared for the confusion and anger that is such a central part of grief. It's a curious thing that, in the west of Scotland, when Catholic family members die those under the age of twenty are more often than not excluded from the funeral and the essential process of mourning. My younger brother and I, the youngest of five siblings, were no exception and were kept from the majority of family funerals until our mid teens. It was being part of SAM that taught me how to grieve.

I quickly became a key member of SAM's squad of volunteers and part of the team that ran the Safer Sex Roadshow, a mobile exhibition that toured around nightclubs, universities, community groups and conferences spreading the word about AIDS, HIV and safer sex. It was useful training for an extremely outgoing and shameless eighteen year old (and a perfect apprenticeship for the work I do now with Terrence Higgins Trust). I was a useful addition to the team, being an exceedingly approachable bundle of testosterone who floated through life dressed like a character from a Tom of Finland drawing. I wore my formative influences on my sleeves, in crop t-shirts that flaunted my six pack and whatever was snaking down the front of my jeans. You'll all be relieved to know that these days my tailoring is a little more modest.

When I turned nineteen, I was fast-tracked onto the Buddy Programme, a scheme whereby SAM linked someone living with HIV with an understanding and informed individual who could be there as a friend or confidant. My first client was a very tall, lanky good-looking young man from Cumbernauld whose cheerful demeanour increased the more unwell he became. He ultimately wanted to see our friendship in more intimate terms, which became too uncomfortable for me, and he was assigned another buddy. He died less than a year later.

My second client was an inmate at Barlinnie Prison who had been convicted of armed robbery. He was bisexual and a drug user. My fortnightly visits to him still give me the chills.

Nothing quite prepares you for being admitted into one of the most notorious of Britain's Victorian jails, even when you know that you're being let out in an hour. After my third or fourth visit, SAM's funding was pulled and given to a new, rival organisation. (The ramifications of that decision still sit uncomfortably with me, and I hope they also sit uncomfortably with those who took that decision, but that goes beyond the remit of this piece.) It meant that I never got to see him again, and to this day I have no idea what happened to him. I hope that he felt the sun on his face and that he managed to find some kind of balance in his life.

The staff at SAM were all dedicated, driven individuals and there wasn't one I didn't immediately love. Funnily enough, the only one with a real sense of reserve was Steve Retson, the manager of the Glasgow office who posthumously gave his name to Glasgow's sexual-health clinic for gay men. Steve was a silver-haired, perma-tanned Scotsman with the kind of camp authority I associated with Larry Grayson (a camp English comedian who was haughtily effete but could silence rowdy audiences with a well-delivered put down and an icy-cold glare). Let's just say he didn't suffer fools. I don't recall exactly when Steve stepped down from the job because of his health, but I remember slowly recognising the tell-tale signs of illness in his face and on his skin, and his trips into the office became fewer. His funeral was a packed affair, and the eulogy was expertly delivered by SAM's chairman and founder, the handsome and very brilliant QC, Derek Ogg, a man who would later become one of my closest friends. SAM drew me to it because it was an organisation with heart, and everyone present at that funeral felt that. Unfortunately, hearts stop beating, and like so many things precious to me at the time, such was the case with SAM. But many of the people I met at SAM, particularly Derek, became permanent fixtures in my life, and I carried the lessons I learned there with me into a new phase of life.

The turn of the century saw me evolve from a gangly, quiffy and utterly naïve lad into a confident, muscular, shaven-headed and successful homosexual about town. I was successful both professionally and sexually, and I found myself inexplicably attracted to, and attractive to, a class of man who can best be described as huge knackered muscle daddies (HKMDs for short). I had relationships with some of these HKMDs, some of whom were HIV positive. HIV no longer scared me. I felt invincible. Many of my closest friends had become positive, and they shared their stories with me, and I became a confidant to them, much in the same way I had been a buddy at SAM.

In 2009, I met and fell in love with a tall, beautiful man called Charlie, the epitome of the muscle daddy. He really did look like he'd been plucked from a Tom of Finland drawing. Two years in, the relationship fell apart, and I fell apart with it. Every aspect of my life suffered, my mental health completely collapsed and I made very poor choices, some of them under the influence of recreational drugs. I fell temporarily into another gay epidemic: chemsex. This is perhaps not the most appropriate forum in which to discuss that particular modern condition, one generally but not exclusively fuelled by iPhones and controlled substances. Suffice to say that in that bad time, I let my guard slip just once, on the 27th of December, 2011.

I'm a big chap; I've always been able to take care of myself and keep danger at bay. But on the 27th of December, 2011, at around 12.25 am, danger came looking for me, specifically. Danger in this case being the psychotic and perpetually drug-fucked lover of one of my dearest friends. We would all occasionally 'play' and, although we played without condoms, I had my limits and they included parameters around sexual contact with men who were HIV+ with a detectable viral load. The chemically fuelled lifestyle of my friend's lover meant that not only was he positive, but also very, very detectable. I'd often have to push him away with force to put my point across. He was always miffed and would send me messages about wanting to fuck me and... well, you can imagine the rest.

On the 27th of December, 2011, I received his special Christmas gift. Can you guess what I got? It wasn't a puppy. At the home of my friend, his lover, he joyfully administered what I thought was a solution of amphetamines, but which immediately turned out to be something quite different. The next hour or so is a blur, and the closest analogy I can draw is with the classic scene from the film *Rosemary's Baby*, where Rosemary is being raped by the devil, and she slowly comes round to the realisation that the staring yellow eyes looking right into hers are not a figment of her imagination. She blurts out, "This is no dream! This is really happening!" Yeah, that's pretty much what it was like. When the lights came up, my arsehole looked a bit like an autopsy. There was a lot of blood and a lot of semen and quite soon thereafter a lot of adrenaline. I showered, cleaned myself out, and came round a bit more. He thanked me. I picked him up and physically threw him out into the street.

I knew what had happened. Rape is an uncomfortable word at any time, but guys who looked like me, guys built like me, guys with my confidence in the bedroom, guys like me who could throw their assailants into the street, didn't get raped. Wrong. I began seroconverting in March 2012, and I knew exactly what was happening. I was eventually diagnosed the day the London Olympics opened. I cried for about ten minutes and then went to the gym. The first person I met was my friend Derek Ogg, founder of SAM. It all seemed to come full circle. He held me and told me it would be fine. And it was, largely.

I was and am enormously blasé about my HIV. I have no option but to embrace it as the nasty, unpleasant, permanent house guest it is, one who initially left soiled underwear in the washing basket and tell-tale splashes of vomit on my slippers. These days, it's learned some manners and is much less chaotic and more orderly—most of the time. Talking about HIV is no problem, but being raped? ...It was four years before I was offered a rape counsellor. I'm still coming to terms with that.

I don't look back at the halcyon days of SAM with any sense of nostalgia or longing, only a longing for those who aren't here and for the unabashed honesty of the time. Because of what SAM taught me, I've thrown myself headlong into activism and trying, for the most part, to be a responsible grown-up gay. I'm happy, I'm engaged, I'm much more sorted. As a jazz musician, and given the title of this piece, there really is only one song to quote to attempt to find a suitable ending: "These fundamental things apply, as time goes by."

Human Rights

Human rights are the basic rights and freedoms that we are all entitled to, regardless of nationality and citizenship. In the UK, human rights are protected by the European Convention on Human Rights, and further protections are included in The Equality Act 2010. These protections offer people living with and at risk of HIV protections against discrimination when accessing healthcare, public services or in employment on the basis of their HIV status or perceived risk. Most recently, HIV Scotland used protections in the Equality Act to argue against discrimination in aviation, which prevented people living with HIV from becoming pilots. This discrimination was successfully overturned.

Ashes of a Visible Girl

Angie Spoto

+

I ground my kneecaps to dust
with running, carelessly
launching myself from the sprinters'
blocks, worried more for the black stubble
sprouting from my ankles, my nails
unpainted, gone rough and grey
from the tarmac
than for my bones

my future bones
now more like saplings
green and soft, bending
under the weight of fruits
ripening the size of melons
stretching my emerald insides
until I feel the dirt beneath
my fingernails and realise
I've hit the bottom

the bottom of prerogative
of the freedom to stretch
without groaning
to get up and *walk*
without hitching

to walk and walk
and dance along
candy pavements, sugar streets
rainbow swirls of slick sweets
hard like teeth, without
a thought for my bones
as if my bones don't exist
as if my body is *not a thing*
because if it's not hurting
it's not there, and now
it is always there, existing
too much

too much to be invisible
again. I have become a stone
among soft bodies, birds
with both their wings
and in my haste to jump
from buildings I've dropped
my rosy glasses. for the first time
I can see the new colours
of a different kind of living:

you've worn the wrong dress
to a party and when other
guests see you they only see
the fabric coating your bones
and every word dropped
from your lips is a gumdrop
of acid—you can never say
the right thing because no one
is listening, they are too busy
side-stepping, pretending
your dress isn't making
them uncomfortable

there are others here who
have stepped into the wrong
clothing. I see that
now. although my bones
have gone to ash for one reason
and not another, I am glad
that I can see them, the others
and hear their words
without worrying
I'm getting burned

Invisibility in Four Acts or Much Ado about Nothing

Will Dalgleish

+

Act I

I'm sure you have heard the expression 'You represent me when you leave this house'? Hmm. Perhaps I jump ahead of myself.

I was brought up in a humble, loving home by hard-working parents who had a liberal outlook on life. I did well at school. Yeah, I was prefect and head boy—Swatty McSwat who, according to others, was a 'poof'. I had no idea or inclination that I was attracted to the male sex (on reflection, there might be a tiny credibility gap there) so I became the quiet one as I didn't want to be bothered or bullied by "them". I behaved myself nearly all the time and wasn't into alcohol or rebelling or drugs, and as it turned out (and much to my surprise... really!) I wasn't into girls either!

My life was okay, until of course I was dragged out of the closet at the tender age of nineteen.

I had been brought up with the question echoing in my head: 'What would the neighbours say?' So, after having learned hard lessons at school, I decided it was time to become even more discrete. I mean, what would they say behind their twitching net curtains of suburbia or, for that matter, what would be said behind the veil of secrets in my own loving home? (Let me explain those twitchy curtains because many have stood and rubber-necked behind them, looking, judging, watching the street and neighbours for some gossip!)

Would I bring shame or dishonour to my family? (I sound like a Klingon, *Qapla'!*) I had real anxiety about this for about the next five years before I learned of gay nirvana. The pull of a gay man's heaven was strong with this one, so after growing some, I moved to London when a career opportunity presented itself.

It was an easy way out for a gay man at that age. I could become invisible, and, no, I don't mean in the Harry Potteresque sense. I ran. No drama, no romanticism. I could happily become invisible.

Act II

London and the gay scene opened its sybaritic arms and welcomed me into its terribly empty heart. I could lift the veil (I'm not exaggerating, alas, as I'm always the groomsman never the groom) and have a good look around. I was as nervous and jumpy as a virgin at his first Highland games.

I suppose, really, I was one of the lucky ones. I began to consider myself an average MSM (men who have sex with men). I experienced no bullying or threats, nor was I called any disgusting terms like 'poof' or 'shirt lifter' or 'fudge packer'. In fact, I had arrived! I had a very good job, began to nurture fantastic friends, holidayed well, visited family often and could hide amongst the rest of the gay community in London. What a huge success! Life couldn't be better?

I could remain invisible, which was something I had worked towards when I first came out in Edinburgh.

Act III

Then it happened. I got the worst news or, as it was at that time, a death sentence; my (now) cherished and unique virus came to join me in my journey through life. Dum dum duuuuuum!

The net-curtain effect had returned to haunt me as well. It had a direct influence on how I related to my diagnosis. At that time there were few or no services after a diagnosis, no support of any type. My friends were helpless as they only saw the tragedy. Stigma and discrimination were very much alive, well and thriving at a time when I was most vulnerable and, tragically, the discrimination I did receive was from my own peers. I remember, when trying to negotiate sex with someone, I was told, "Why don't you go die of AIDS?"

Things like that, the press, keeping it quiet, and maintaining a smile on my face (without Botox!) and internalising—because that was all I knew—had a devastating effect on me. Not just in how I related to my family and friends, but on my mental health and familial and romantic relationships. I battled with self-destructive behaviour and low self-esteem, and even now I still struggle with an ability to form meaningful intimate relationships.

I was with the love of my life (up till now) for a number of years and we both found it difficult to talk about my status. I remember saying, "You know I probably won't make old bones." To which he replied, "I have a family history of Parkinson's" which somehow led to further silence and, I might add, rather good rumpy pumpy. What I'm trying to say is: I couldn't communicate with him about it and he didn't know how to reciprocate, which ultimately led to the breakdown of something which should very much be alive and thriving (much like my gorgeous self).

I lived with the virus (that messy bloody flat mate who leaves everything behind them and doesn't care of the effect on those around... not recommended!) and the disability it caused. I had interventions to correct lipoatrophy, which then went terribly wrong and involved eleven subsequent maxillofacial surgeries to correct what, to my eyes, looked like someone else's face. In fact, I think someone mentioned I looked like Sideshow Bob (minus the hair—oh, and the makeup).

So, in the very act of trying to fit in and not look like someone who was positive, I ended up even more damaged and reclusive. Any exclusion was based on the way I felt people looked at me! My thin veneer had cracked, and I looked different; I didn't fit in. I wasn't the whole package. I never quite fitted the archetypal success-driven gay man due to my one (fatal) flaw. This had the knock-on effect of exacerbating my own self-directed hate and stigma which fuelled a lack of self confidence. My reclusiveness made me feel almost entirely transparent and very much alone!

A little bit of me died every time I was rejected because of my status because, ultimately, I perceived it as a rejection of me as a person. Did I become reclusive, self-destructive and unlovable because of my status? I think I'll be paying my therapist for many years to understand that one.

I was among loving friends and family, but I had become invisible.

So that's all a bit shit, eh?

Act IV

Thankfully, now nothing is as it was before.

I first need to take you back two years ago, when there was a perfect storm of events which led me into activism and advocacy for those living with and at risk of HIV. Becoming an activist was another life-changing event, but this time no threats of a terrible end to life or burning in hell. (By the way, if you end up there, the next pit over will have a great party going on. Come over!)

In fact, my activism almost, but not quite, cancels out all the crap that went before. (Hmmm, on further thought, the negotiating sex bit can still be problematic, and I know you'll be very surprised to hear I'm still single. I know. I am surprised too. But my cup runneth over in other areas of my life, and that's not a euphemism, folks.) The catalysts that led me to activism are numerous and too many to mention.

What's that I hear you say? Oh, okay then, just a couple of examples.

The word 'catharsis' is an appropriate term to express what I have gone through. (Even writing this has given me a further sense of empowerment.) I had met with other positive people, and suddenly I could share my story in a safe place and realise that others have gone through what I have. It made me feel less alone. Their journeys are as unique as mine, and because of this sharing, my self confidence returned. I'm now happy to share my story with at-risk communities, basically anyone who'll listen, so that we can reduce or maybe even eradicate stigma, and, ergo, new infections

I also told a group of my work colleagues around the same time. It was a huge gamble, even with rising confidence, and you know what? They listened. They were interested and wanted to know a lot more, so of course I didn't hold back.

Me: "I'm HIV positive."

Them: "Okay, really ... Tell me more ... I'm interested ... Where can we find out more? ... Is there anything we can do?"

Me: "Nerdy nerdy nerdy nerdy blah blah HIV education blah blah stigma blah blah nerdy nerdy."

I now have a little more faith in the human condition. I have begun to trust others again. (No, that doesn't mean I'll be asking others to buy a fascinator just yet.) I'm not silent about HIV any more, mainly due to the encouragement of (some very special) people who I hold very dear. (Boak! Don't you just hate public displays of affection?)

That damn net curtain still affects people's lives whether real or perceived. Of course, combine that with the genuine fear of disclosure and you probably have one of the main stumbling blocks in our fight to reduce and eradicate this bloody annoying, now middle-aged, virus.

I have removed and burned my net curtains. I want to tear down that thin veneer of acrylic that shades others, and I say *Pah* to stigma and discrimination.

This is my dreadfully beautiful virus which I control. It doesn't control me (as much) anymore. I have a healthy outlet to express a side to myself which I had hidden. I take joy being the 'community activist' and being controversial and using my big gob to push and cajole and council and consult and contribute and change!

Hi! My name's Will and I just happen to be HIV positive!

Curtains up, light the lights, hear the sounds of outrageous applause, resounding cheers and trumpets playing!

Ta Dah!

I'm definitely not invisible anymore!

Ageing

Thanks to effective medication, people living with HIV are living longer, healthier and happier lives. Ageing does, however, bring challenges to everyone. The need to ensure social-care services are fit for purpose, free from discrimination, is important for people living with HIV. The impact of long-term medication can also cause problems for people ageing with HIV, especially if someone requires treatment for additional conditions. Ensuring people age well with HIV is a major priority for HIV Scotland, and work is underway to ensure all services meet the needs of people living with HIV as they age.

Contributors

RJ ARKHIPOV is a poet, conceptual artist and translator of homosexual literature whose work treats the breadth of the contemporary gay experience. In September 2015, he performed and exhibited Words&Blood—a poetry series written using his own blood as ink—at the CRISIS performance arts festival in Paris. Arkhipov's first collection of poems, essays, and photographs—*Visceral: The Poetry of Blood*—explores themes of abjection, ancestry, faith, intimacy, mortality, and stigma through the poetics of flesh and blood.

MARK CARLISE: I am 54 years old and have lived in Dundee for eleven years. I grew up in Liverpool and have always enjoyed writing poetry and short stories and find it a very useful for helping me to deal with my emotions. Since I contracted HIV in 2005, my writing has provided me with an invaluable outlet for all the pent-up emotions that I have had to contest with. It also allows me a very good method of escaping the confines of solitude and isolation that having a positive diagnosis can bring.

KEVIN CROWE was born in Manchester in 1951 and worked in factories and pubs, until going to university as a mature student, afterwards working in social care. For most of the 1990s he was employed by local authorities as an HIV, Aids and sexual-health worker. In 1999, he and his partner, Simon Long, moved to the Highlands to open a bookshop and restaurant. In 2005, they entered a civil partnership and, as soon as the law allowed, converted it into marriage. A life-long socialist, Kevin has throughout his life been involved in campaigning groups. He has had fiction, poetry and non-fiction published in many magazines, anthologies and online outlets.

WILL DALGLEISH fell asleep at 30 and wonders how he woke up one morning to be 52. He loves the roller coaster of life— learning and challenging, loving and caring. His family and friends bring him joy. He considers every day to be a school day. Oh, and he loves *Star Trek*!

STEPHEN DUFFY is a jazz vocalist and radio broadcaster, presenting BBC Radio Scotland's *Jazz House* programme since 2007. Nominated for a Sony Radio Academy Award, he has performed with the Scottish National Jazz Orchestra, the BBC Radio Big Band and the London Gay Big Band, with whom he enjoys an especially close association. He is also a coach for young and aspiring jazz vocalists. An advocate for those living with and affected by HIV, he has also worked in this sector with a number of national organisations. His hobbies include bodybuilding and being nice.

J. WILLIAM JAMES is a Scottish-Irish writer who was raised in Edinburgh. He graduated from Oxford University in 2013 and now lives in London. He is working on his first novel, set in the same world as 'Víreas'.

Matthew Lynch: I was diagnosed with HIV around November 2017. The transition wasn't difficult as I was diagnosed early, but the daily routine of taking medication created some anxiety. I wanted to create imagery reflecting that.

James McAbraham AKA James Shearer-Bromfield attended Banchory Academy, Aberdeenshire where his interest in poetry began. He cites Norman MacCaig as influential.

Son of Glaswegian Alex Shearer and an English mother, who divorced when he was young. He knew he was gay at school when it was still illegal in Scotland. Devoted to his stepmum Mairaed on Skye, he respected his Aberdonian stepdad, Ian Bromfield.

"HIV diagnosis, rapid impact, was a chaff and wheat separation process, and I am grateful to Kevin and my LUL boss Steve Charlick and other friends for being there."

He is a Liberal Jew.

NJ MILLAR came to Glasgow for a party thirteen years ago and never left. She has worked in the arts ever since. This will be her first published work.

NOBODY has written this poem with the hope that it might help somebody.

MICHAEL NUGENT is a Glaswegian born and bred. A man with many talents (sarcasm being top), he is a designer and teacher by day and a 24/7 HIV advocate and positive person living every moment to its fullest.

Oliver: I'm a 27 year old who's been living, working and recovering in Edinburgh for just over a year. I've used drawing as a way of coping during times of severe mental illness, and lately I've been using my creative skills to express my personal experience of the world we live in. Last year, I exhibited my first photography piece about mental illness and have been finding myself focusing more on LGBTQI craftivism this year. I'm not sure where it's taking me, but I will continue striving for social and political change, and raising awareness of issues that matter.

Rio: I've lived in Scotland, Nigeria, London and France. In France, my premature baby died at six weeks of an infection in hospital. I turned to heroin to block the hurt.

I'm nearly 60 and have been diagnosed over half my life. I am delighted at all the improvements in treatment; I would like to help get through to people that stigma can be more damaging than trying to deal with the illness.

My kids are my world. Stigma affected their young lives, and I hate that. I'd love to help normalise HIV and let people know not to rule out being parents because of a diagnosis.

FRASER SERLE is Anglo-Scots. He was born in London and raised in Edinburgh. He was diagnosed with HIV in 2005. Fraser has spent the last 28 years in England, working in both paid and unpaid capacities within the HIV and sexual-health sectors. In 2010, he left the NHS and set up as an independent public-health practitioner. 2010 was also the year he decided to give something back, becoming a peer mentor at Positively UK, where he is currently a trustee. Fraser likes maps, flags, stamps, social justice and hot men with beards. He recently moved back to Edinburgh.

NATHAN SPARLING is the Head of Policy & Campaigning at HIV Scotland as well as being a PrEPster and a drag queen. Previously he worked as a senior advisor in Westminster for the SNP, with a focus on social-justice policy. He was born in Glenrothes.

ANGIE SPOTO is an American fiction writer and poet. Her most recent endeavours include a lyrical essay about her Italian family, a collection of horror surrealist fairy tales, and a fantasy novel about grief. She is working toward a PhD in Creative Writing at the University of Glasgow and volunteers with the Glasgow-based social enterprise Uncovered Artistry, which supports the creativity of domestic and sexual abuse survivors. She is artist in residence at HIV Scotland. Her work has appeared in *Crooked Holster, From Glasgow to Saturn* and *Toad Suck Review.*

JAMIE STEWART: My life is *way* too complex to sum up in a biography which is less than 15,000 words, but here's a stab: I have worn so many different hats. Some of them the right ones. The latest ('actor') seems to be growing on me.

There's stuff I'm confused and frustrated by in my bio. And definitely still working through. How do borderline personality disorder and HIV and gay intertwine and interact? Working through the shame and stigma of each and all these is a lifetime's work.

Maybe language, words, and storytelling can tame the chaos and bind the beasts. Or at least harness them into a useful sleigh team to pull us out of the dark.

Lightning Source UK Ltd.
Milton Keynes UK
UKHW020432070319
338603UK00008B/78/P